GAME ON!

RACE DOWN THE SLOPES

BY BRANDON TERRELL

12 STORY LIBRARY

www.12StoryLibrary.com

Copyright © 2015 by Peterson Publishing Company, North Mankato, MN 56003. All rights reserved. No part of this book may be reproduced or utilized in any form or by any means without written permission from the publisher.

12-Story Library is an imprint of Peterson Publishing Company and Press Room Editions.

Produced for 12-Story Library by Red Line Editorial

Photographs ©: Dreamstime, cover

Cover Design: Nikki Farinella

ISBN
978-1-63235-050-3 (hardcover)
978-1-63235-110-4 (paperback)
978-1-62143-091-9 (hosted ebook)

Library of Congress Control Number: 2014946084

Printed in the United States of America
Mankato, MN
October, 2014

TABLE OF CONTENTS

CHAPTER 1

FIELD TRIP!

"Oh man, what am I doing?" Fourteen-year-old Gabe Santiago looked down at the pink permission slip in his hands. He'd almost told his friends that he'd forgotten about it or that his parents hadn't signed it. That way, instead of spending the afternoon with his classmates out at Mount Grove, the ski hills located just outside of town, he could sit in an empty classroom with the few other kids who didn't care for skiing or snowboarding.

An empty and warm classroom, Gabe corrected himself.

He and his friends were lined up outside of East Grover Lake Middle School, waiting to board a series of buses that would whisk them away to Mount Grove.

"Come on, it's gonna be fun," Ben Mason, one of Gabe's best friends, said. He nudged Gabe from behind.

"Ben, winter sports and I go together like orange juice and brushing your teeth. I haven't been skiing that often."

"Lighten up, dude," Logan Parrish, another of Gabe's good friends, said with a smile. Logan had a black snowboard with a bright blue snake on it tucked under one arm. "By the end of the day, you'll be King of the Bunny Hill! I'll make you a crown and everything."

Ben and Logan laughed. Gabe didn't appreciate their joke. He tugged at the sides of his red stocking cap.

"Smile, guys!" Annie Roger wielded a large camera at the three friends. "Get in close and pretend you like each other." Ben and Logan squeezed in on either side of Gabe as Annie snapped a few shots.

She peered over the camera at Gabe. "What's the deal, Gabe?" she asked. "Turn that frown upside down, dude."

Gabe forced himself to smile. It felt uncomfortable.

"What's with the photos?" Ben asked.

"Oh, I'm taking a few shots for the *Grizzly Pages*," Annie explained. The *Grizzly Pages* weren't actually made of paper. It was the name of the middle school's student-run news website. It was mostly about sports and school events. Currently, the top story was about Coach Horton and the boys' basketball team getting second place in the conference finals.

"Okay, everyone! Have your permission slips ready, please!" At the front of the line, near the door of the lead bus, stood Mrs. Hartley, the school's civics teacher and coach of the alpine ski team. Over her head she waved a permission slip identical to the one Gabe was fretting about.

Mrs. Hartley was one of the younger teachers at East Grover Lake. Gabe was in her third-period class.

The line of kids, all in thick winter coats and snow pants, began to file into buses. Some of them—like Ben and Logan—brought their own equipment. Gabe would rent gear at Mount Grove.

By the time Gabe and his friends climbed aboard the bus, they had to sit near the front. Ben and Logan sat together and talked about how awesome it was going to be to shred down the advanced hills. Annie sat next to Gabe.

As the bus rumbled away from the curb and they began their jouncing journey, Gabe heard the unmistakable laugh of Eliza Monroe behind him.

Gabe craned his neck to look for her. Sure enough, Eliza was seated in the back of the bus. She was propped up on one knee and leaning her back against the windows. Eliza's bubblegum pink coat was adorned with lift passes from Mount Grove. She was a natural on the slopes, a member of the school's alpine team.

Cassie Flock, one of Eliza's best friends, was sitting with her. They laughed again, Eliza throwing her head back.

"Whatcha looking at?" Annie asked. She followed Gabe's gaze. "Ohhhhh."

"What?"

"Eliza Monroe." Annie smirked.

"What about her?"

"Oh, come on, Gabe. It's totally obvious. You've got a crush on her."

Gabe shook his head. "Do not," he said.

"Pfft! Of course you do."

Of course he did. He just didn't want to admit it to his friends. Besides, he didn't expect Eliza to like him back. She revolved in another social circle entirely. For a brief moment in time, though, during football season, he and Eliza had spoken to one another. Since then, though, it was like she didn't even know he existed.

Gabe slouched down in his seat and sat quietly for the remainder of the bus ride. He used one glove to scrape the frost from the inside of his window and stared out at Grover Lake as the bus drove through town.

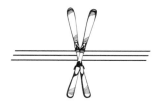

Finally, the bus turned into the parking lot for Mount Grove. Gabe saw the sign by the road, two mountain peaks carved into a square hunk of wood, shaped like the "M" in

Mount Grove's name. The excitement in the bus ramped up as kids prepared to shove and jostle their way down the narrow aisle.

"Here we go!" Logan said, rubbing his hands together like a maniacal super-villain about to unleash a devilish plan on an unsuspecting hero.

Gabe followed his friends into the aisle. His boots clunked down the steps and onto the hard-packed snow. He looked up at the massive hill in front of him. It was filled with powder and trails and trees and ski lifts and people carving their way from the peak to the bottom, and he muttered under his breath, "Oh boy."

CHAPTER 2

AN OLD ENEMY

The chalet at Mount Grove was a two-story building. On the first floor was a rental counter and a locker room lined with banged-up blue lockers. The second floor consisted of a cafeteria.

Gabe's first stop after getting his lift pass was the rental area. A man in his 30s, with a beard and a pair of thick glasses, passed Gabe a set of old white skis and poles, a pair of boots, some goggles, and a helmet.

Gabe carried his gear outside. Logan and Ben already had one foot strapped into their snowboards. They stood near one of the chairlifts, pointing up at the nearest trail.

"Ready to go, Gabe?" Annie asked. She was securing her helmet. A device, almost like a miner's light, was attached to the front of it.

Gabe pointed at it. "What's that?"

"A video camera. That way, I can get some first-person footage of me skiing down a hill."

"Cool."

Nearby, Eliza Monroe stood with her friends. Her skis were stuck in the ground next to her, and she had one arm around them.

"I think she likes you," Annie said. "You should go talk to her. See which trail she's going down first."

"You think so?"

"Yeah. Go for it."

Gabe balanced his gear in one hand. Then he reached into his coat pocket with the other and brought out his lucky rabbit's foot. Gabe was beyond superstitious. Any chance he had to sway luck in his favor, he took it. He'd brought the white rabbit's foot along to help in his skiing endeavors. He hoped it would work for this, too.

"Okay," he said, "here goes nothing."

He took a deep breath and walked toward Eliza.

"Coming through!" a voice bellowed from behind him. Someone slammed hard into

Gabe's shoulder, knocking him forward. All eyes, including those of Eliza, turned to watch as Gabe fumbled around with his skis. They swung around comically, almost smacking Gabe right in the head. The skis, poles, and helmet rattled loudly and fell into the snow.

"Whoa," said the person who had just plowed into Gabe. "Careful where you're swinging those skis."

When Gabe saw the culprit, his cheeks flushed with anger. It was Jacob Fuller, a tall and athletic teen who went to their rival school, West Grover Lake. Gabe and his friends weren't exactly members of the Jacob Fuller Fan Club.

The West Grover Lake teen sneered at Gabe. Then he said, "Hey, Eliza. Looking good. You girls ready to show off your moves?"

Embarrassed, Gabe scooped his things off the ground and sulked back toward Annie, Ben, and Logan.

Gabe tried to forget his literal run-in with Jacob Fuller by taking the chairlift up the hill. He and Annie rode together. The chair was rickety, and there were no bars to lock them inside. With the weight of his skis on his feet and the swaying of the chair, Gabe felt like he was going to fall out. He gripped the side of the chair fiercely.

How do people think this is fun?

At the top of the hill, he managed to stay upright as he slid down off the chair.

Annie came to a stop beside him. "Which trail do you want to try?"

Gabe looked around. There were about five trails nearby. Two had blue square signs, signifying they were intermediate runs. Two others were marked as black diamond trails, the most difficult.

Gabe pointed to a circular green sign. "That one," he said. Green trails were the easiest.

Annie lowered her goggles. "Follow me." She clicked on the camera strapped to her helmet and a little red light began to glow.

Gabe pushed off with his ski poles, gliding across the snow to the start of the trail. It looked like a straight, relatively smooth run.

Maybe this isn't so hard.

He leaned forward, began to slide down the hill, and let gravity take over.

CHAPTER 3

CARVING OUT SOME FUN

Gabe carefully controlled his descent down the green trail. He carved slowly back and forth. He was actually doing fairly well, but ahead of him, Annie was moving expertly down the trail. Gabe quickly fell in behind her.

Other skiers zipped past him, fearless kids who didn't care about speed. He saw one boy farther down the hill take a wild tumble, losing his skis. As Gabe passed him, the kid sat up, laughing.

Gabe was halfway down the trail when he thought, *Let's see what happens if I pick up the pace.*

He leaned forward and instantly felt the change. It was as if the skis were pulling him down the hill. He bent his knees and tucked his poles under his arms.

He caught up with Annie easily. "Whoa!" she shouted, surprised to see him whiz past her. "Wait up!"

But Gabe couldn't. He was barreling down the hill now. He approached another teen, a snowboarder, leaned left, and blew by him. He didn't feel out of control, though. He actually felt pretty good, like he was getting the hang of it.

Halfway down the hill, that all changed. He hit a small hill called a berm and shot into the air.

"Ahhhh!" Gabe waved his arms like a frantic bird. His skis hit the powder again, blasting up a spray of white. He wobbled left, then right, but maintained his balance.

I'm still skiing, he thought, shocked. *How am I still skiing?!*

Gabe managed to make it all the way without crashing. As he reached the bottom of the hill, though, he realized that he didn't know the best way to stop. He twisted his body as he'd seen Annie do, bringing his skis perpendicular to the hill in a "hockey" stop.

The edge of his front ski caught in the hard-packed ground, and his uphill ski and leg smacked into it. Gabe lost his balance and toppled over. He struck the ground, the impact driving the air from his lungs. He landed on his back and slid across the ground a bit before coming to a stop.

"That could have gone better," he croaked to himself.

Gabe, dazed yet exhilarated, wiped the snow from his goggles and stared up at the blue, cloudless sky.

Annie glided over to his side and pried her goggles off. She leaned over him, blotting out the sun. "You okay, Gabe?"

Gabe laughed. "Never better. That was awesome!"

Annie helped him to his feet and brushed snow from his coat. "You wanna go again?"

"Absolutely!"

The two friends skied together for the remainder of the afternoon. After executing a few more runs on the green trails, Gabe was feeling like a natural on the ski slopes. So they decided to try a tree-lined intermediate blue trail. Annie skied behind him to capture Gabe's run on video.

He sailed down the hill, the cold wind biting against his cheeks. The blue trail wound around to the left, meeting up at the bottom with several others next to a chairlift. As Gabe neared the lift, he thought he spied Eliza's pink coat in the crowd.

Gabe was determined not to crash in front of the crowd. He made a large-radius turn, keeping his skis parallel, and pressed his booted heels down perfectly. This time, his hockey stop was flawless.

Annie peeled off her helmet and clicked the red button on her camera. "That was fantastic!" she said. "I can't wait to watch the footage."

Gabe smiled. He glanced over and saw that, indeed, it *was* Eliza in the pink coat.

And she was looking right back at him.

"Nice run, Gabe," she said.

Gabe was struck silent. His mouth was dry, lips chapped. His tongue felt like it was made of cement.

Annie nudged him in the back.

"Uh . . . *gracias*," he said.

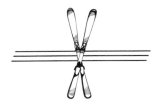

CHAPTER 4

A RASH DECISION

The following morning, as Gabe climbed onto the bus outside his house and took a seat with Logan, the boy in front of them turned and said over the seat, "Hey, Gabe. Sick moves yesterday."

Puzzled, Gabe muttered his thanks.

And then, as he and Logan walked into the school and met Ben in the cafeteria, another group of kids complimented his skiing from the day before.

"Okay, what's going on?" he asked his friends.

"Didn't Annie tell you?" Ben handed Gabe his phone with the video already uploaded. "She posted this last night."

On the screen was a header for the *Grizzly Pages*, its name written in a bold red font. The school's mascot roared behind it. Below the header was a video clip with the caption "Gabe Santiago Shows Off His Moves During Class Field Trip."

"Oh no," Gabe said.

He pressed the button and watched the video clip. It was shaky and at times hard to see, but Annie's helmet camera did a pretty good job of capturing Gabe's fantastic run on the blue trail the day before, right down to his near-perfect stop.

"I'm bummed Logan and I were snowboarding on a different run and didn't get to see this firsthand," Ben said.

"I thought you didn't like skiing," Logan added.

Gabe shrugged. "It turned out to be pretty fun." He looked around to make sure no one was listening and then added, "Also, I had no idea what I was doing out there."

Logan and Ben laughed.

All morning, Gabe was met by classmates who offered their opinion on Annie's video. Gabe was surprised at how quickly the video had gone viral. And how many of his fellow students thought he actually knew what he was doing out on the slopes.

At lunch, Gabe sat down at his usual table. His grandmother, an excellent cook, had packed his lunch, as usual. In his brown bag that day was a thick turkey-and-Swiss sandwich, dried apples, and a pair of homemade gingersnap cookies, Gabe's favorite.

He laid his food out in front of him as Ben sat down on the other side of the table. His tray rattled as he dropped it. On it was nothing but a slice of greasy pizza.

"Lunch of champions," Gabe said sarcastically.

Ben wiggled his eyebrows and took a huge bite. Cheese oozed down his cheeks. "Better believe it," he said with a full mouth.

Annie and Logan soon joined them. As Gabe was about to take a bite of his delicious sandwich, a voice behind him said, "Hi, Gabe."

He nearly dropped his turkey and Swiss.

Gabe turned in his seat. Eliza stood, her hair tucked behind one ear, hands on her hips. She wore a thin sweater with a gray button-down shirt underneath, and a long, flowing skirt.

"Huh . . . hi," Gabe managed to utter.

Usually, a gaggle of girls surrounded Eliza like Secret Service agents protecting the president. Now, though, she stood alone.

"I saw the video from yesterday," Eliza said. "You're a natural on the slopes."

"I am?"

"You are."

"I am."

"Have you skied your whole life?"

Gabe thought a moment, and then, inexplicably, answered, "Yes. Kind of."

Annie kicked him in the shin under the table, but Gabe ignored the pain.

Eliza smiled. "I thought so. Well, I just wanted to let you know that the ski team is looking for a couple more people this season. Greg moved and Hattie broke her arm this past fall. You know, if you're looking for something to do this winter and want to ski with us."

Ski with Eliza? Be around her every day?

Before Gabe knew what he was doing, he blurted out, "Sure! Sign me up!"

Eliza smiled from ear to ear. The strand of hair being held back by her ear fell loose as she stepped forward and placed her hands on Gabe's shoulders.

"Yay," she said. "I'll tell Mrs. Hartley. It's gonna be fun. I promise."

"Okay." Gabe's heart was beating so hard, he thought it was going to crack a rib or something. He watched Eliza walk over to her table of friends and slide into a seat. She didn't look back, just jumped right into the conversation.

"Joining the ski team, huh?" Logan asked.

"I guess so," Gabe said quietly, thinking, *What am I doing?*

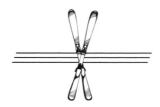

CHAPTER 5

WELCOME TO THE TEAM

"I'll see you after practice, *nieto*!"

Gabe's grandmother Rosa waved as he climbed out of her rusty, dented sedan. She wore her uniform for the Lake Diner, where she worked as a server. She had brought him out to Mount Grove after her lunch shift.

Gabe opened one of the back doors and grabbed a pair of skis, boots, poles, and a helmet off the seat. The equipment was old; his uncle Ernest had used them as a boy, and his grandma just happened to still have them up in her attic.

"*Gracias, abuela.*" Gabe slammed the door closed and gathered his things.

His grandma honked the car's horn and drove off.

It had been a couple of days since Gabe had agreed to join the alpine ski team. He'd talked with Mrs. Hartley and had signed the appropriate paperwork.

All because of a girl, he thought as he took in the towering ski hill before him.

The team met in the chalet's cafeteria. Gabe dropped his things in a rack outside the building and looked around for Eliza. He figured she must be inside.

The team consisted of about 20 kids total. Eliza stood with Kelsey Hartford and Cassie Flock. Gabe recognized many of the other team members from class. Nathan Millett sat in a chair talking with Mrs. Hartley. Chase Overbrook, whose black hair was gelled up in a wavy spike, was listening to music through a pair of oversized, expensive headphones.

There were also several skiers who Gabe didn't recognize. In fact, he was pretty sure they didn't go to his school, but rather to West Grover Lake Middle School. The two schools must have been combined to create the ski team.

Gabe stood back quietly, not speaking with anyone.

What am I doing here? I totally don't belong.

He was actually thinking about cutting out when Eliza saw him. She waved, and his pulse quickened.

"Hey, Gabe." She motioned for him to join her. He did. "You guys know Gabe, right?" she asked Kelsey and Cassie, and even though Cassie was his lab partner in biology, it took her a second to nod her head.

"I know Gabe!" A kid sitting nearby turned in his chair, and Gabe saw Jacob Fuller for the first time. Jacob smiled that smug grin of his and waved. "So you're our new recruit, eh?"

Gabe's heart sank like the *Titanic*. "Yeah," he said, "that's me."

"Oh, so you guys know each other already?" Eliza asked.

Gabe sighed. "Yep, sort of."

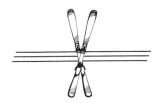

Mrs. Hartley spoke briefly to them. "Good afternoon, everyone," she said. Her voice was light and airy. "Our first meet is here next week, so today's practice will be less about practicing your slalom and giant slalom techniques and more about familiarizing yourself with the slopes.

"There is a new member among us," she continued, pointing to Gabe. "Gabe Santiago, from East Grover Lake." The team turned to look at him. Gabe shrugged back. "Welcome, Gabe, and let's hit the slopes, everyone."

Gabe followed the team outside again and began to strap on his equipment. He looked around at all of the new, sleek gear

worn by the other skiers. Nathan's left
ski alone probably cost more than Gabe's
grandma's car.

As he pushed off toward the chairlift,
Chase buzzed past him. "Welcome to the
team," he said as he zipped along.

Gabe rode the chairlift alone to the top.
There was no Annie this time to calm him
down. His nerves were in overdrive.

He decided on a blue trail known as the
Dogleg, because of the way it took a hard left
turn halfway down the mountain. Other team
members took off down black diamond trails.
He saw Chase expertly push off down the
mountain's hardest trail, the Black Mamba.

Gabe took it easy for the first few runs.
He wanted to familiarize himself with all of
the trails before speeding down them. When

he did let loose and start to gain momentum, it felt amazing.

He was halfway down his third run on Dogleg when he sensed someone approaching from his left. It was Jacob Fuller, carving down the hill with ease. He skied close to Gabe, too close for Gabe's comfort.

Oh great.

Without a word, Jacob turned left, kicking up a huge spray of powder in his wake. It flew up into the air, striking Gabe and making it impossible for him to see. Gabe stumbled and felt himself falling in slow motion.

He hit the snow hard, skipped back into the air, let go of his poles, and braced himself for impact. He struck a snowdrift, tumbling like a tennis shoe in the dryer. His boots came free of their bindings, and his skis skittered down the hill. The strap of his goggles snapped, exposing his eyes. He squeezed them shut.

When he came to a stop, Gabe was off to the side of the trail. He lay on his back, arms and legs spread wide, like he was about to make a snow angel. Jacob hadn't even looked back.

"Yep," Gabe said, groaning and sitting up. "Welcome to the team."

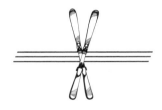

CHAPTER 6

A FAMILIAR FACE

"They call this a 'yard sale,'" Nathan Millett explained, scooping one of Gabe's ski poles off the ground, where it had come to rest against a tree trunk. "Because all of your equipment is scattered around the ground like junk at a yard sale."

Gabe had been lying in the snow for a minute or two before Nathan had skied down Dogleg. He'd pulled up and stopped, unstrapping his skis and helping Gabe to his feet.

"*Gracias*," Gabe said. He stretched his arms over his head. He was sore from falling, but that feeling was dwarfed by his anger at Jacob Fuller.

Gabe plucked his goggles out of a snowdrift. The strap was indeed broken, and there was a large crack in the plastic.

"Looks like I'm hitting the rental shop," he said.

Nathan helped him strap his skis back on. Instead of barreling down the course, Gabe was tentative. He stuck with the snowplow move, where he angled his skis in a "V" shape and slowly descended the hill. It didn't help that he wasn't wearing goggles. His eyes watered and he had to squint. The wind biting against his skin felt like pinpricks.

When he reached the bottom of the hill, Gabe unstrapped his skis and propped them up in the rack outside the chalet. He hooked his helmet next to them. Despite the cold, his forehead was sweaty, and his curly brown hair was tamped down on his head.

The rental shop employee was the same bearded guy as last week. This time, though, he was not alone.

Carrying a large cardboard box marked "DONATE" was another bearded man, one whom Gabe immediately recognized.

"*Hola*, Sal!"

Sal Horton was the burly owner of Sal's Used Sporting Goods in downtown Grover Lake. Sal's shop was cluttered with sports equipment, shelves stacked high, glass cases filled with signed baseball cards and footballs and all kinds of memorabilia. Gabe and his friends visited the shop often, and Sal had a knack for knowing just what they needed.

"Afternoon, kiddo," Sal said. He set the box on the floor beside him.

"What are you doing out here?"

"Dropping off a few things for the rental shop. I don't have room for them anymore."

I believe it.

"What about you, Gabe?" Sal asked.

Gabe held up his goggles. "I need a fresh pair."

"On it," the bearded guy said. He began to head toward the back room, but Sal stopped him.

"I'll get them, Patrick," Sal said.

"Sure thing, Pops."

Pops?! I didn't know Sal had a son.

Come to think of it, the guy working the rental shop *did* look quite a bit like Sal.

Sal stepped briefly into the back room. When he emerged, he was twirling a pair of orange goggles on one of his meaty fingers.

"Here you are, Gabe," Sal said. He passed over the goggles. They were fairly new, with only a couple of scuffs on one side.

Gabe turned them over in his hands, examining them. "Cool. Is there anything... *special* about them?" Usually, when Sal offered a piece of equipment, there was a story or purpose behind it.

Sal smiled. "Well," he began, "they're orange. Does that count?"

"Oh." Gabe's heart deflated. Then, quietly, "Thanks, Sal. Patrick."

He turned and began to head back outside. "Say, Gabe," Sal added. "I've got a few more things to drop off tomorrow. See you then?"

"Yeah. Sure."

Gabe stepped outside, slid the new goggles on, strapped his skis to his boots, and pushed off for the nearest chairlift.

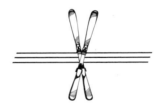

RIV
TEA

Gabe found hi
No sense i
Wanted

When he reached the top of the mountain and slid from the chairlift—he was actually getting the hang of it—Gabe spied Eliza up ahead with Cassie. They waited at the start of a blue trail named Eagle Pass.

Eliza saw him, too, and waved. "Hi, Gabe," she said. "Wanna join us?"

"Sure."

He'd tried Eagle Pass a couple of times, but he wasn't entirely familiar with the run. As they started down the hill, Eliza to his left, nself pulling back on his speed.

careening down the course; he

to enjoy skiing beside his crush.

As the course slowly turned to the right, Eliza hit a soft berm and briefly caught air. She kicked her skis up and then back down to nail the landing.

Whoa. Impressive.

Gabe hit the same spot just after Eliza. Instead of any fancy moves, he opted to play it safe so he could avoid winding up with another "yard sale" on his hands.

He landed hard but bent his knees to absorb the shock.

Eliza twisted her head around to watch Gabe, and he saw a wide smile on her face.

When they reached the bottom of the run, Eliza said, "Should we go again?"

Gabe didn't even hesitate. "Yeah."

They rode the chairlift together to the top. Eliza sat close enough that their legs brushed against one another. Gabe was both extremely happy with the situation and so freaked out he almost wanted to leap from the lift.

"I'm glad you decided to join the team," Eliza said when they were halfway up the hill.

"Thanks. I am too."

"I know we don't really talk in school. Which is crazy. You and your friends seem really cool."

Gabe nodded. "Yeah. I'm glad we changed that."

"Me too."

They looked at each other, and the way their eyes met made Gabe's heart skip a beat.

The moment was fleeting, though, as they'd reached the top of the lift.

The two headed back toward Eagle Pass for a second run. Tailing behind them this time was Jacob Fuller.

"Gabe!" he shouted. "Did you enjoy the *trip* you took last *fall*?" He chuckled at his own terribly clichéd joke.

Gabe hoped that if he ignored Jacob, the bully would leave them alone.

He didn't. Jacob broke away from his friends to follow Gabe and Eliza down Eagle Pass.

He carved down the hill on Gabe's left side. When Jacob would ski close, their poles nearly tangling together, Gabe would force himself to the right, closer to Eliza, out of the way.

"Knock it off, Jacob!" Eliza's words of warning were nearly lost in the rush of wind.

Gabe and Jacob hit the berm in the center of the run at the same time. They exploded into the air. Gabe, the more compact and lighter athlete, soared a bit farther than Jacob, landing several feet in front of his rival. The powder sprayed up in Gabe's wake caught Jacob by surprise. He shielded his face with one arm, nearly losing his balance.

With renewed strength, Jacob barreled down on Gabe. Gabe skied as fast as he ever had before. Eliza was farther up the hill, safe from the dueling teens.

As they reached the bottom of the hill, Gabe twisted his body left to brake. In doing so, he cut right in front of Jacob. Jacob lost his balance. One of his poles stuck in the snow. He wobbled back and forth before crashing in a big, snowy heap.

Gabe chuckled as he shed his skis and walked over to Jacob. "I'm sorry. You okay?"

Jacob slapped Gabe's offered hand away. "Get away, dude," he said, lumbering to his feet. "You're dangerous."

"Hey, that's not any worse than what you did."

In response, Jacob shoved Gabe hard in the chest.

"What's going on here?" Mrs. Hartley scurried across the snow.

Gabe's breath hitched in his throat. He hadn't been hit that hard since football season. Then, he'd at least been wearing pads.

"I just . . ." Gabe stammered, "We were racing, and—"

"And Santiago cut in front of me, like he was trying to make me fall," Jacob lied. He also neglected to mention that he'd done the same thing earlier to Gabe.

"Remember," Mrs. Hartley said, "we're not enemies here. We're all on the same team. Please act like it."

Gabe felt awful. He really wasn't trying to hurt Jacob. As Mrs. Hartley walked away, Gabe tried to apologize. "Look, Jacob, I'm—"

"Shove it," Jacob said, gathering his things and stalking off toward the chalet.

CHAPTER 8

A NEW WAY OF SEEING THINGS

True to his word, Sal Horton was waiting for Gabe outside the chalet the next afternoon. He sat watching skiers race down a nearby hill. His massive figure was perched atop a picnic table, and in one hand was a mug of something steaming hot.

"Looks like you'll be practicing slalom racing today," Sal said as Gabe approached. He nodded up toward Dogleg, where a series of poles and flags were placed in a zigzag formation along the run. A couple of skiers were already weaving their way between them.

"Huh. I've never tried it before," Gabe said.

"Are you enjoying skiing with your new team?"

Gabe shrugged. "Yeah. I kind of actually love skiing, which I never thought I'd hear myself say. I'm not as skilled as my teammates, but mostly I'm just trying to find my own style, I suppose. Yesterday wasn't a very good day, though."

"Because of your crash? The one that broke your goggles?"

"That, and I nearly got into a fight with Jacob Fuller."

"I see." Sal was aware of the unfriendly behavior Jacob had exhibited toward Gabe and his pals in the past.

"He didn't like how I was skiing."

Sal lumbered to his feet. "Follow me," he said, leading Gabe into the rental shop. Patrick was there, prepping a set of charcoal gray skis. "Patrick, could you hand me the item I brought with me today?" Sal asked.

"Sure thing." Patrick reached under the counter and snatched out a pair of goggles. They were sleek, with a red frame and a reflective lens that seemed to shine gold in the light.

"Goggles?"

"Yes," Sal said, "only this pair used to be worn by Bode Miller."

Patrick tossed the lightweight goggles over to Gabe. Gabe didn't know much about skiing and snowboarding, but there were a few athletes he was familiar with. Lindsey Vonn. Ted Ligety.

Bode Miller was another.

"You and Mr. Miller appear to have a lot in common," Sal said.

"Because of all the Olympic medals I've won?" Gabe joked.

"You both ski with a certain . . . passion. Medals don't seem to be the ultimate goal for Mr. Miller. He's often reckless, risking his chances to crash just so he can win."

"He's said his goal is to 'ski as fast as the natural universe will allow,'" Patrick added. It seemed Sal wasn't the only Horton full of information.

"Huh," Gabe said, looking down at the goggles in his hands.

"Don't worry about what others think of you, Gabe," Sal said. "Just be yourself, and you'll do great."

"Thanks." Gabe waved the goggles in front of him. "And thanks."

"Any time," Sal and Patrick said in unison.

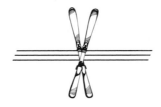

When Gabe stepped out of the warm chalet and into the cold again, he saw the crowd of people right away. They were huddled together near the base of Dogleg.

Eliza was there. Nathan Millett. Even Jacob Fuller.

"What's going on?" Gabe asked Eliza, trying to see what all the fuss was about.

Mrs. Hartley was in the middle of the group. "Everyone take a step back," she ordered them. As they did, Gabe peered between his teammates to see Chase Overbrook lying in the snow. He was clutching an ankle, grimacing in pain. Mrs. Hartley knelt beside him.

"Oh no," Gabe whispered.

CHAPTER 9

VOLUNTEER

Eventually, the members of the ski team, as well as a few other curious bystanders, backed away from the fallen Chase and stood near the chalet. Gabe and his teammates watched in silence as a ski patrol medic joined Mrs. Hartley. Together, they examined Chase's ankle and leg.

"I can't believe it," Eliza said. "Chase is our best skier. He could win the slalom on one ski."

Mrs. Hartley and the medic were able to help Chase to his feet. The teen tried to place weight on his injured foot, but he couldn't.

"You'll need X-rays for sure," Mrs. Hartley said. "Let's get you into the chalet until your parents get here." Nathan Millett offered his assistance, sliding Chase's arm over his shoulders. The medic did the same, and together they helped Chase into the chalet.

When they were inside, the team immediately gathered around Mrs. Hartley. "What are we going to do?" Cassie asked.

"Chase is our best skier," Eliza repeated.

Mrs. Hartley raised her hands to silence them. "Relax, everyone. Yes, it appears that Chase will be out for some time this season. Which means we will need to fill his spot for the slalom for our next meet."

The team looked around at one another. Though there were almost two dozen of them, only five boys and five girls were allowed to compete in each event. Gabe's status as a "newbie" meant he wouldn't be asked to race at his first competition.

At least, that's what he thought.

"Gabe could take his spot," Eliza said, volunteering him.

What?!

Everyone turned to face him. Mrs. Hartley tilted her head to one side in consideration.

"I . . . I . . . couldn't possibly fill Chase's ski boots," Gabe said.

"No, but you can certainly race," Eliza said. "I've seen you. I know you can do it."

"Would you like to try the slalom, Gabe?" Mrs. Hartley asked.

Eliza's belief in Gabe made his pride swell. As before, because somehow the beautiful blonde had a knack for getting Gabe to push himself, Gabe blurted out, "Sure."

Mrs. Hartley clapped. "Okay, then it's settled. Everyone back to work, please. Gabe, partner up and practice on Dogleg."

"Yes, ma'am."

"I'll be his partner," Eliza offered.

Mrs. Hartley shook her head. "No, I think I'd like to pair Gabe up with Jacob today."

What?! Gabe thought.

"What?!" Jacob said.

"You're competing in the slalom event at the meet, Jacob. I'd like you to work with Gabe so he can practice it as well."

"Yeah, okay," Jacob muttered. He strapped on his skis and said, "Come on, Santiago."

Gabe hurriedly attached his own skis and slid the pair of Bode Miller goggles over his eyes.

This is going to be awesome, he thought sarcastically.

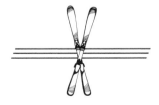

The ride up the hill on the chairlift was chilly and silent.

When they reached the top, Jacob pushed off for Dogleg without a word. Gabe followed.

"So what's with the gates?" Gabe asked.

Jacob glared at him. "You gotta be kidding me," he said. "I thought you'd done this before."

"Oh. No, I totally have," Gabe said, floundering. "I was just . . . it was a joke."

"Sure. Lead the way, then."

Gabe looked down at the red and blue gates staggered along the trail. He sighed. "Fine. You got me. I have no idea what I'm doing."

"Figures." Jacob pointed down the hill. "The purpose of slalom is to weave around the gates. They're closer together than they would be on a giant slalom course. The turns are quick, so you're going to have to watch your speed, and always keep your eyes on the next gate. Here. Watch."

Jacob took off down the hill. He hit the first gate and turned abruptly, keeping his skis parallel to one another. Gabe watched Jacob repeat this action until he was just a tiny figure at the bottom of the course.

"Well," Gabe said to himself, "here goes nothing."

He crouched low and began his run. To his surprise, he curved nicely around the first gate.

Hey! Not so bad, he thought.

Until he totally missed the second gate.

He tried to rally, fighting his way into the middle of the course, back to the gates. Jacob was right; the turn radius was tight each time.

Jacob waited for him at the bottom of the hill, hands on his hips.

"That was ugly," he said.

"Thanks, Captain Obvious," Gabe said.

They rode up again, but this time Jacob proceeded to offer some advice. "Try to stay in the fall line," he said, referring to the imaginary line that provided the straightest route down a hill. "Your ski edges are super important. Try to hit the gates with your shins. Keep low and you'll turn faster."

The second time down the hill, Gabe managed to hit the first three gates. The time after that, he hit five. He practiced until his legs burned, his muscles being pushed further than they'd even been pushed before. He was determined to hit every gate.

On his eighth time down, he almost nailed it. It wasn't pretty, but he successfully navigated the course, everything except the last gate. He immediately hit the chairlift.

I can do this.

On his last run of the evening, as the sun set behind the hills and left a burning orange sky in its wake, Gabe made it down, hitting every gate on the course. Jacob Fuller was waiting for him at the bottom.

"I think you're getting the hang of it," Jacob said as Gabe brought his skis to a stop.

And then Jacob Fuller did something Gabe had never once seen him do before: he offered Gabe a high five.

CHAPTER 10

THE BIG MEET

On the day of the big meet, Gabe rode with the team out to Mount Grove. Most kids were quiet or wearing headphones and listening to music. Gabe sat by himself, one hand clutching his lucky rabbit's foot, the same charm he had carried on the field trip. That felt like an eternity ago.

Ten teams were competing in the meet. An enormous crowd was gathered at the chalet, where teams signed in and skiers waited to take their turns on the course.

Annie, Ben, and Logan burst out of the crowd as Gabe approached. They waved frantically to get his attention.

"Good luck," Ben said.

"Ski like the wind!" Logan shouted.

Gabe rolled his eyes.

"Don't let them psych you out," Annie said.

The Grover Lake ski team huddled together, and Mrs. Hartley handed out numbers to each racer to pin to his or her coat. "Today's event will be a little different," she explained. "Usually each racer gets two runs, but because of the Dogleg's length and the number of competitors we have at this meet, you will only get one. So make it count."

Nathan and Cassie were in the first group of skiers. Nathan ran the course perfectly, coming in with an impressive time: 1:10:23. Cassie did well, too, leading the girls' scores by almost a whole second at 1:13:09.

"Great job," Mrs. Hartley said. "In alpine skiing, every fraction of a second counts."

She was right; in the next group of skiers, a boy from Kingston beat Nathan Millett's time by one-thousandth of a second, taking the lead away from Grover Lake.

Jacob Fuller did his best to get the lead back, but he missed by a half-second. Gabe couldn't believe that he was *actually* cheering on his old nemesis.

Finally, it was Gabe's turn. As he was about to push off toward the chairlift, a voice behind him said, "Good luck, Gabe."

He turned to see Sal and Patrick standing in the crowd.

"Knock 'em dead, kid," Patrick added.

Gabe smiled. "Thanks, guys."

He rode the lift with a girl from Valley Hill. They were both quiet, thinking more about their upcoming run than about small talk.

At the top of Dogleg, a small station had been set up. Gabe checked in with the officials and then waited until his name was called. When it was, he skied over to the starting line at the top of the hill.

He stared down at the course, at each gate, remembering every move and turn from his practice runs. Adrenaline coursed through his veins, making him feel almost electric. He saw the crowd at the bottom.

The official nearest him squeezed the trigger on an air horn, and Gabe was off.

Gabe shot down the hill toward the first gate. Before he'd even reached it, he was thinking of gate number two. He struck the first one perfectly. Then he cut left, his skis slicing into the hard-packed snow.

The second gate rushed up to greet him, and his shin slapped against it. Gabe was in the zone. It felt like he was carving down the slope at breakneck speed.

The third gate whizzed past him in a blur, and he headed for the fourth.

Gabe continued down the course with razor-sharp focus. He had nothing to prove; he was, after all, the least qualified to even be racing. But he thought of Eliza, of his friends cheering him on, and the drive to succeed grew strong.

With three gates left, Gabe was looking great. He was sure to get his best time ever. Then, as he passed the next gate, his inside leg hit a rut in the snow, and he began to wobble.

Oh no!

Gabe struggled to maintain his balance. His calf and thigh muscles were on fire. His legs were turning into jelly.

Come on! he thought. *Don't lose it now!*

Somehow, miraculously, he stayed up. He whisked past the gate, just barely clearing it.

The last two gates gave him no problems. Gabe leaned forward and cruised past the finish line.

The crowd erupted in cheers. Gabe came to a stop. He dropped his ski poles and pumped his fists in the air. Annie, Ben, and Logan broke free from the crowd. They surrounded Gabe, offering him hugs and high fives.

Gabe peeled off the goggles once worn by Bode Miller and stared at the leaderboard. As he did, a deep voice said, "Time for Gabe Santiago, Grover Lake: 1:11:17."

"Whoa!" Gabe blurted out.

"That puts you in fifth place!" exclaimed Annie.

"Great work, dude!" Ben slapped him on the helmet.

Eliza came over, leaping with joy. "That was such a great run," she said. "I knew you could do it, Gabe." Then she leaned over and pecked him quickly on the cheek.

Gabe almost fell over in the snow.

The remainder of the Grover Lake team commended him on his run, and Mrs. Hartley said, "You're a natural on the slopes, Gabe. I'm so glad you decided to join the team."

"Me too, Mrs. H.," Gabe replied.

As the meet continued, Gabe's place in the standings dropped. When all was said and done, he finished in twelfth place individually. The team, however, finished in third place. They stayed at the chalet until long after the other teams had packed up and rumbled away in buses. Gabe found himself recalling every detail of his run to his friends and teammates. Cassie's eyes grew wide as saucers as Gabe described losing his balance.

"Okay, everyone!" Annie shouted. "Huddle up for a team photo." The Grover Lake alpine ski team stood together, side by side, as Annie lined up the shot.

"Santiago!" Even though they were sort of friends now, Jacob Fuller's voice still made Gabe jump. "Over here!"

Jacob pointed to an open spot between him and Eliza.

"A photo of Gabe standing next to a smiling Jacob Fuller?" Gabe heard Logan say. "That's like getting your picture taken with Bigfoot."

"Okay, everyone smile and say *cheese!*" Annie shouted.

"Cheese!"

Click!

THE END

ABOUT THE AUTHOR

Brandon Terrell is a Saint Paul-based writer. He is the author of numerous children's books, including picture books, chapter books, and graphic novels. When not hunched over his laptop, Brandon enjoys watching movies and television, reading, baseball, and spending every spare moment with his wife and their two children.

ABOUT THE SKIING STARS

Bode Miller has been part of the U.S. Ski Team for nearly two decades, and he's one of its most successful skiers ever. He has won six Olympic medals.

Olympics: 1998, 2002, 2006, 2010, 2014

Olympic Medals: 1 gold, 3 silver, 2 bronze

World Championship Medals: 4 gold, 1 silver

Lindsey Vonn is probably the most successful female skier to ever wear the red, white, and blue, and in 2010 she became the first U.S. woman to win Olympic gold at a downhill event.

Olympics: 2002, 2006, 2010

Olympic Medals: 1 gold, 1 bronze

World Championship Medals: 2 gold, 3 silver

Ted Ligety appears to be fearless in the way he skis, and it shows in how he attacks giant slalom courses. He also is the only U.S. men's skier to win two Olympic gold medals.

Olympics: 2006, 2010, 2014

Olympic Medals: 2 gold

World Championship Medals: 4 gold, 1 bronze

THINK ABOUT IT

1. Motivation is the reason a character does something important in a story. What is Gabe's motivation for joining the ski team? Use examples from the story to explain your answer.

2. Gabe and Jacob Fuller are from rival schools. Does your school have a rival team that it competes against? Or does your favorite sports team have a rival? Is it good to have a rival? What sort of effect does playing against a rival have on how well or how hard a team plays?

3. Gabe carries around a lucky rabbit's foot with him in *Race Down the Slopes*. Read another Game On! story and see if Gabe has any other lucky charms. What role does luck play in each of the stories for Gabe?

WRITE ABOUT IT

1. Even though Gabe is afraid at first, he seems to have a knack for skiing. Have you ever been scared to try something, whether a new activity or a new food, and afterward found out you enjoyed it? Write a story about what happened.

2. Gabe and Jacob Fuller don't like each other at first, but in the story Jacob actually helps Gabe learn how to slalom. Have you ever been in a similar situation where you had to do something with a person you didn't necessarily like? Write a story about it. Did everything turn out okay in the end?

3. Have you ever wanted to be an Olympic athlete? Describe the event that you would compete in and tell why you think you would do well in this event.

GET YOUR GAME ON!

Read more about Gabe and his friends as they get their game on.

Eyes on the Puck
Goalie Annie Roger learns she needs prescription glasses, and her confidence is shattered. Will a visit to Sal's Used Sporting Goods be enough to help Annie see things differently?

Pass for the Basket
When a new transfer student takes away the spotlight, Ben Mason is frustrated with his role on the basketball team. Will Ben be able to learn the true meaning of leadership?

Strike Out the Side
Logan Parrish has a great fastball, but hitters are starting to figure him out. After a devastating loss, Logan goes searching for a new pitch. Will it be enough to help Logan in the big game?